ALICE DALGLIESH

THE
LITTLE
WOODEN
FARMER

PICTURES BY ANITA LOBEL

The Macmillan Company, New York/Collier-Macmillan Limited, London

Copyright 1930 by The Macmillan Company
Copyright renewed 1958 by Alice Dalgliesh
Copyright © Anita Lobel 1968
All rights reserved. No part of this book may be
reproduced or transmitted in any form or by any means,
electronic or mechanical, including photocopying,
recording or by any information storage and retrieval
system, without permission in writing from the Publisher.
The Macmillan Company, New York
Collier-Macmillan Canada, Ltd., Toronto, Ontario
Library of Congress catalog card number: 68-12081
Printed in the United States of America
New Edition, 1968

First Printing

for Jennifer Dalgliesh

Once upon a time there was a little wooden farmer who lived with his little wooden wife in a neat wooden farmhouse. It was a nice farmhouse with a bright red roof and green trees growing beside it.

Beside the house was a barn, by the barn was a pigpen, in front of the barn was a place where sheep might be kept, and at the other side of the house was a dog kennel.

"It would be the nicest farm in the world if only there were some animals to live on it," said the little wooden farmer to his wife.

"The nicest farm in the world," answered the little wooden wife, who always agreed with everything her husband said.

Now the farmhouse was on a hill, and at the foot of the hill there was a river which curled and twisted through the green fields like a ribbon. Every day a wooden steamboat came along the river and the farmer and his wife stood on their little dock and waved to it. The captain of the boat was very friendly and always waved back.

One day the farmer had a clever thought.

"I shall ask the captain of the boat to bring me some animals," he said. "Somewhere along the river that winds in and out there must be animals that do not belong to anyone."

So the next day as the boat went by the little wooden farmer called to the captain and told him what he wanted.

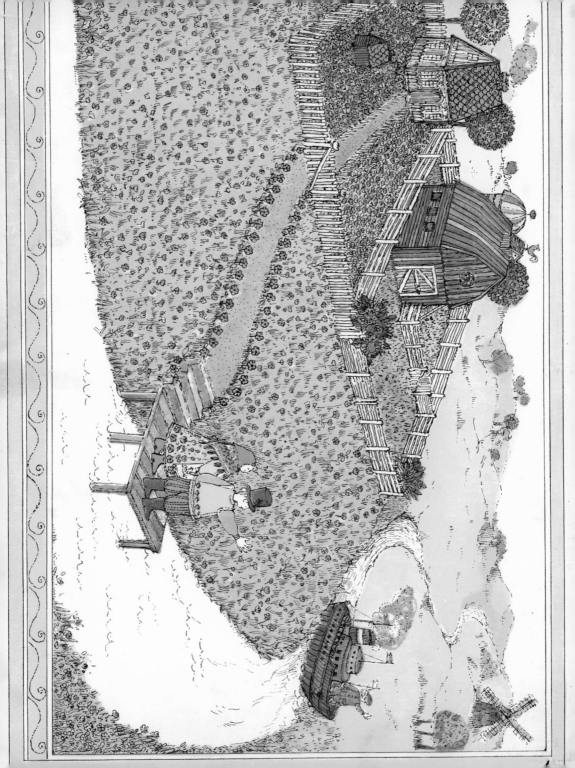

"Oho!" said the captain. "That should be easy. All along the river there are animals that do not belong to anyone. I see them every day."

"Then," said the little wooden farmer, "I should like to have:

a brown cow that gives rich creamy milk,

two white sheep with warm wooly coats,

a fat pink pig with a curly tail,

a rooster that will crow in the morning,

a hen that will lay a large brown egg each day,

a dog to guard my house

and

a cat to sit on the doorstep."

"Very well!" said the captain. "I shall try to remember all those things." As the boat sailed away the farmer could hear the captain saying to himself — "A brown cow — two white sheep — a fat pink pig — a rooster — a hen — a dog and a cat."

The boat had not sailed very far along the river before the captain saw the sheep. They were standing in a meadow eating buttercups and their coats were very white and wooly.

"White sheep!" called the captain. "Come with me and I will take you to a place where you will have a fine home and something nicer than buttercups to eat."

"Ba-aa! We would like that!" answered the sheep. So with a frisk and a prance they came aboard.

The boat had sailed around two curves in the river before the captain found the pig. It was so fat and pink and its tail was so curly that he knew it was just the pig he was looking for. The captain had hardly said, "A good home—plenty of skim milk," before the pig came aboard, puffing and panting and grunting with delight.

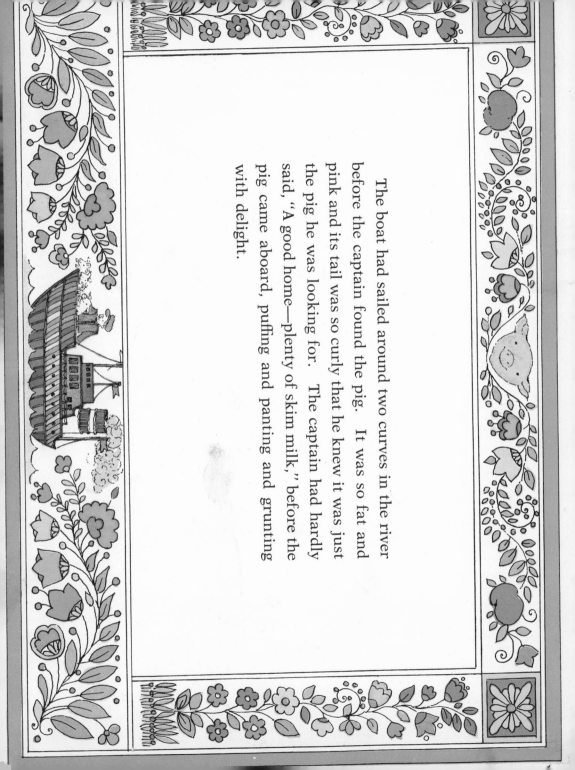

Around the very next curve the captain saw the brown cow. She was standing under a tree doing nothing in particular.

"Brown cow!" called the captain. "Do you give plenty of rich creamy milk?"

"Indeed I do!" answered the cow, with a flick of her tail.

"Then come with me," said the captain. "You will have a fine home in a barn with a bright red roof."

So the brown cow came aboard.

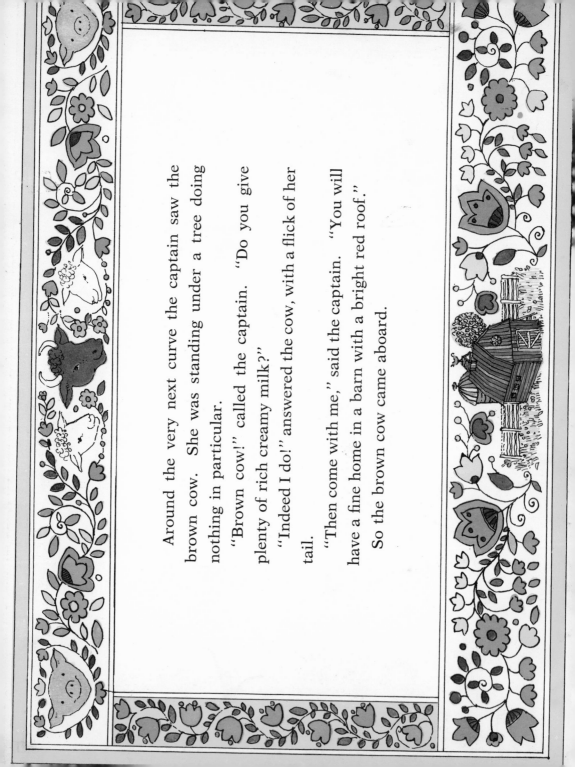

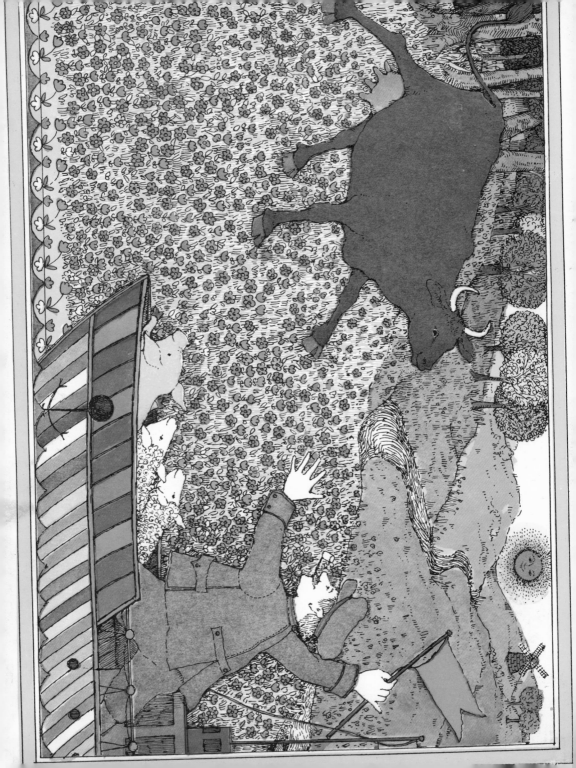

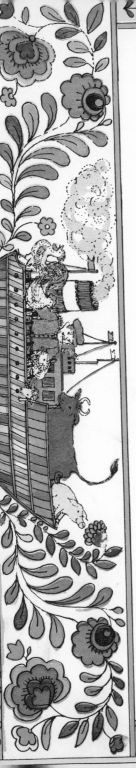

It was quite a long time before the captain found the rooster and the hen. The hen was making such a cackling over a large brown egg she had laid that it was quite hard for the captain to make himself heard.

When at last they did hear, the rooster and the hen lost no time flying aboard. They left the egg behind because the hen said it really did not matter, she could lay another one the next day.

As for the cat and the dog, the captain never did find those though he looked and looked all the way along the river. He even got his telescope and looked through that, but it did not help at all.

"Well, I have done my best," he sighed. "I hope the farmer will not be disappointed."

The next morning the captain saw the little wooden farmer and his wife standing on the dock waiting for him. Beside the farmer stood a little white dog and beside his wife sat a little white cat. "Well, well!" said the captain as the boat came alongside the dock. "I am glad you found the cat and dog yourselves—I found all the others."

"Oh, thank you!" said the little wooden farmer as the captain put down the gangplank.

Over the gangplank walked the brown cow, the white sheep, the pink pig, and the hen and the rooster. The farmer and his wife helped them on to land and showed them their new home.

After that, each day when the boat came down the river the captain would blow his whistle, "Toot! toot!" and all the animals would come to the fence and answer in their own ways.

"Moo-oo!" said the brown cow.

"Ba-aa!" bleated the sheep.

"Oof-oof!" grunted the pig.

"Cluck! cluck!" said the hen.

"Cock-a-doodle-doo!" crowed the rooster.

"Mew! Mew!" said the cat and

"Bow, wow!" barked the dog.

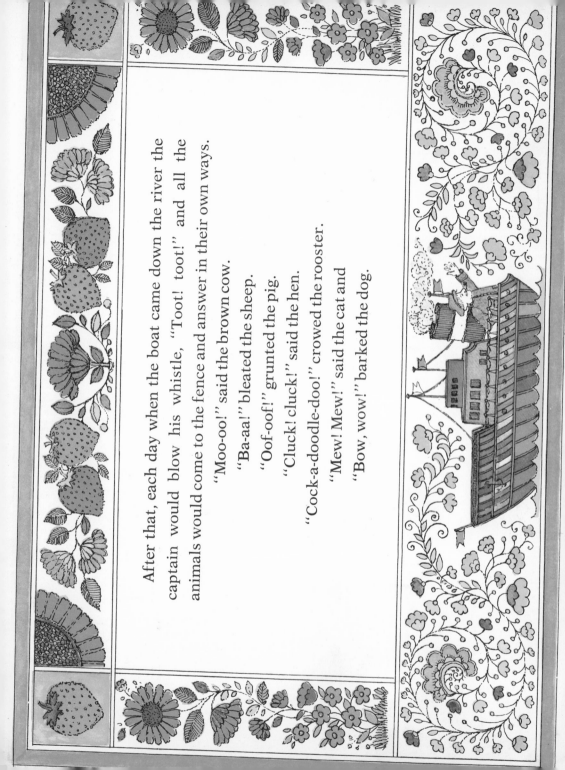

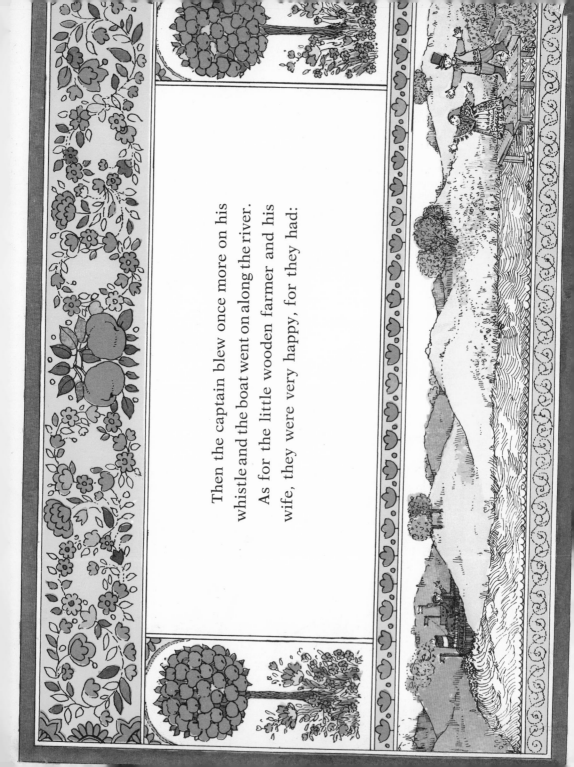

Then the captain blew once more on his whistle and the boat went on along the river. As for the little wooden farmer and his wife, they were very happy, for they had:

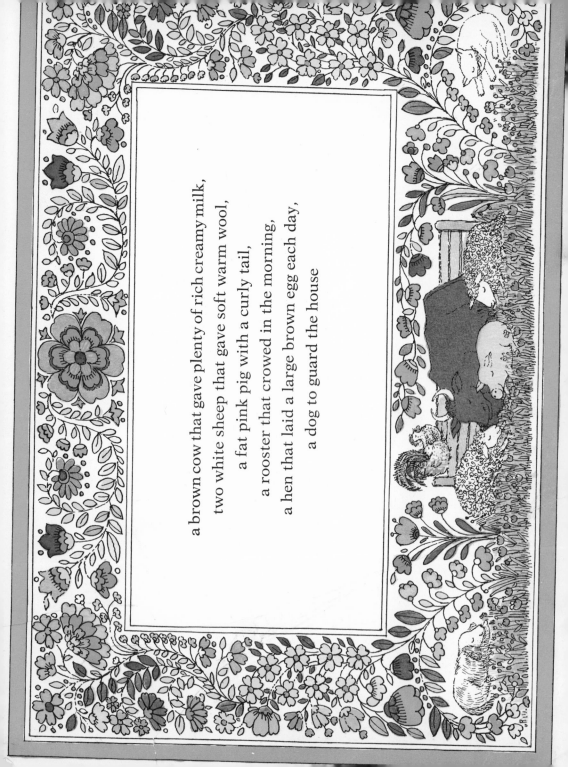

a brown cow that gave plenty of rich creamy milk,
two white sheep that gave soft warm wool,
a fat pink pig with a curly tail,
a rooster that crowed in the morning,
a hen that laid a large brown egg each day,
a dog to guard the house

and a cat to sit on the doorstep or purr by the fire.